this

ORQ.

(he say "ugh!")

David Elliott

illustrated by **Lori Nichols**

troika books

The Turtle Challenge

How many turtles did the artist paint for this book?
The answer is on the inside back cover.
(Hints: In each turtle-fort, find the turtle with the number on it;
it will tell you how many turtles are on that page.
Don't forget the turtles on the cover.
The "tremendous turtle" counts, too!)

This for Rebecca M. Davis.
David say "Fab!"
—DE

For Prentiss.
He top-notch friend.
He fun.
—LN

Published by TROIKA BOOKS
Troika Books Ltd, Well House, Green Lane, Ardleigh, CO7 7PD, UK
www.troikabooks.com

This edition first published 2017 by arrangement with Boyds Mills Press,
an imprint of Highlights Press, Inc. and Highlights for Children International, Inc., USA

A CIP catalogue record for this book is available from the British Library

ISBN 978 1 909991 34 7

1 3 5 7 9 10 8 6 4 2

Printed in Poland

Designed by Anahid Hamparian
The text of this book is set in Neutraface.
The illustrations are done in #4 pencil on Strathmore drawing paper and colourised digitally.

This Orq.

He cave boy.

Wear skins.

No shoes.

Sometimes say . . .

"UGH!"

This Woma.
Best friend.

Every day
have fun.

But cave life tough.

Cold cave.

Dark night.

Raw bison.

And . . .

. . . DORQ!

Dorq big! Orq small.

Dorq hairy!

Orq . . . ?

Dorq strong!

Orq working on it.

Caba no prize either.

Dorq!
UGH!

Caba!
DOUBLE UGH!

Orq's mother give advice.
"If you ignore them, sweetheart,
they'll stop bothering you."

That easy for *her* to say.
Dorq impossible to ignore.
Caba even worse.

Orq catch lunch.
Dorq eat lunch.

Woma find egg.
Caba take egg.

Orq and Woma build fort.
Dorq and Caba *like* fort.

Dorq and Caba mean!
Orq and Woma . . .

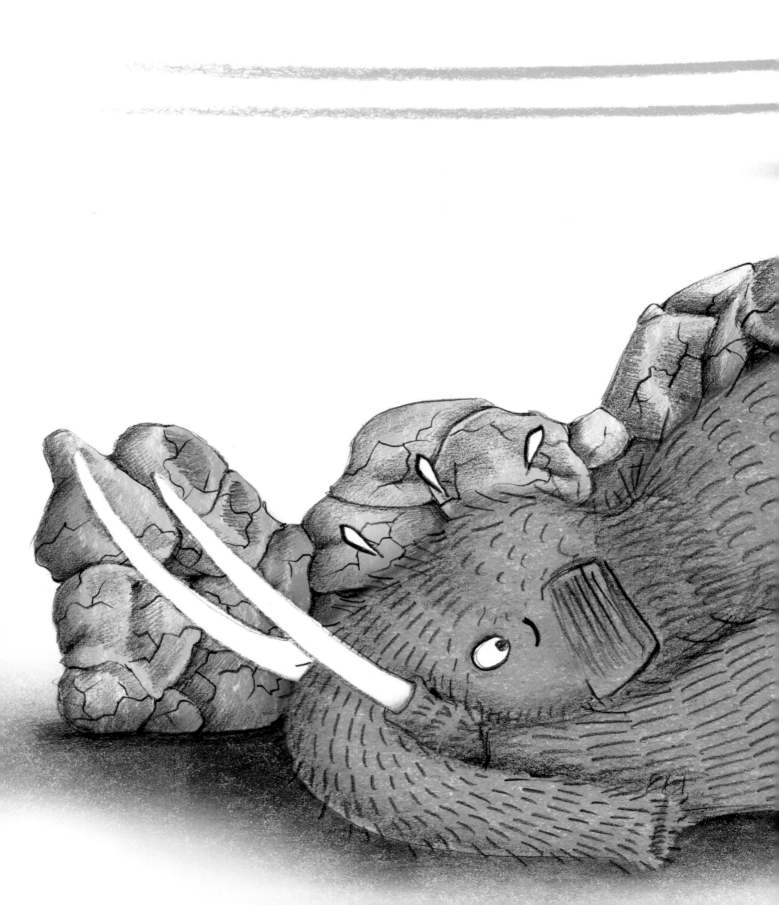

. . . fast!

One day, Orq and Woma hunting.

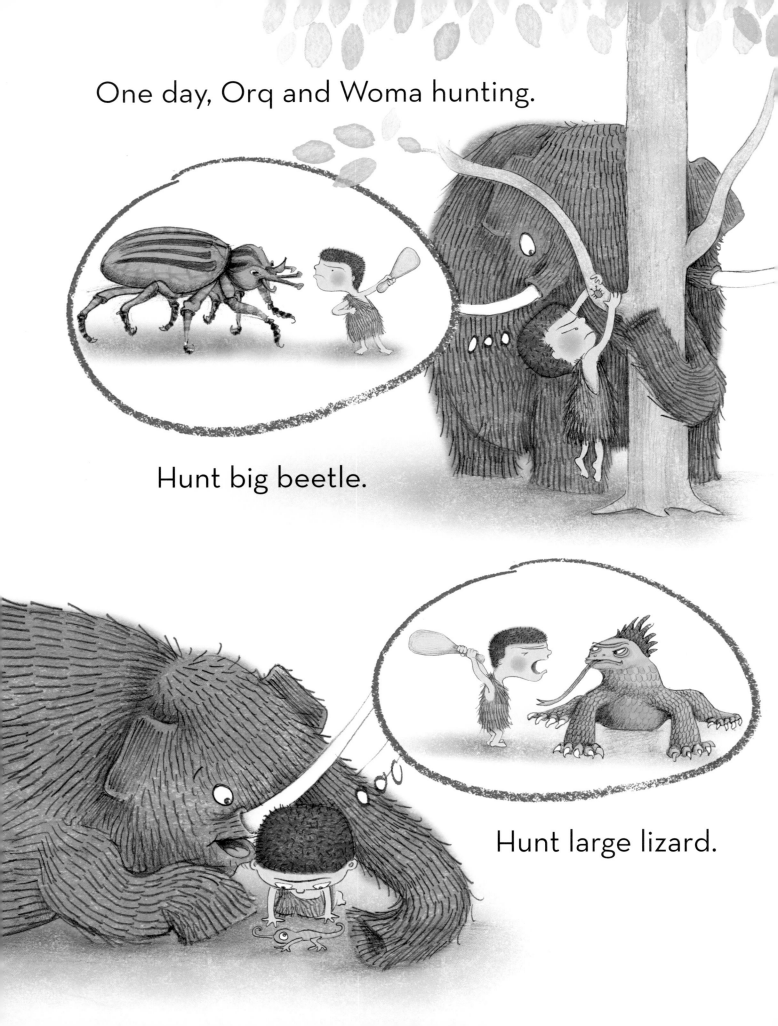

Hunt big beetle.

Hunt large lizard.

Hunt
tremendous
turtle.

Find . . .

. . . Dorq and Caba!

Orq and Woma fast . . .

. . . but not fast enough.

Dorq!
UGH!

Caba!
DOUBLE...

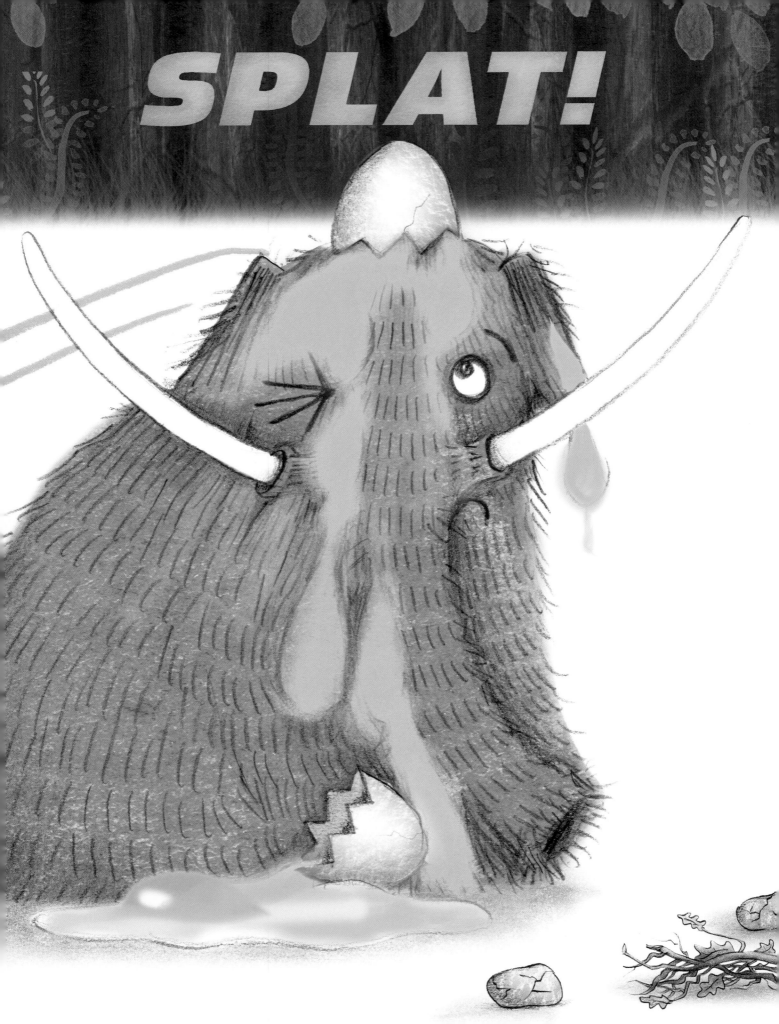

Now Orq angry.

Oh.

Orq discover

FIRE!

Orq Woma's hero.

Orq everybody's hero.

Warm cave.
Night light.
Bison burgers!
YUM!

DOUBLE YUM!